METCALF. Paula   Poddy and Flora

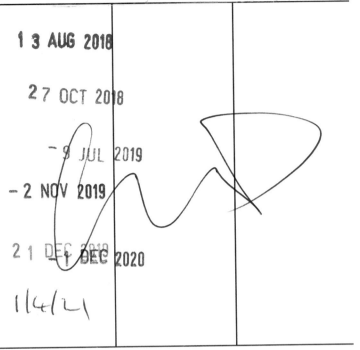

For Freya
And to Leonard who, although a cat,
is my very own Poddy

First published 2010 by Macmillan Children's Books
a division of Macmillan Publishers Limited
20 New Wharf Road, London N1 9RR
Basingstoke and Oxford
Associated companies throughout the world
www.panmacmillan.com

ISBN: 978~0~230~70419~0 (hb)
ISBN: 978~0~230~70736~8 (pb)

Text and illustrations copyright © Paula Metcalf 2010
Moral rights asserted.

1 3 5 7 9 8 6 4 2

A CIP catalogue record for this book is available from the British Library.

Printed in Italy

Poddy and Flora

Paula Metcalf

MACMILLAN CHILDREN'S BOOKS

Some things go very well together, like
jelly and ice cream, like buckets and
spades, and like Poddy and Flora.

Every day during the summer, Poddy and Flora rushed out into the garden to play.

They swung in the trees,

they skipped,

they danced,

and they snoozed in the soft grass.

One morning, Poddy woke up to find Flora was packing a case.

"Hooray!" he thought. "We must be going on holiday."

"Oh Pod," sighed Flora, "you can't come with me to Gran's. Her flat's too small for you and your tail."

Soon it was time for Flora to go.
"Bye bye my beautiful boy!"
she said, and off she went.

It was very quiet in the
house without Flora.

Poddy went outside
to play.

He swung in the trees,

he skipped,

he danced,

and he snoozed in the soft grass.

But it wasn't the
same without Flora.

On his way back inside, Poddy noticed his reflection in the pond. He stopped, he stared. Something was missing!

He checked his eyes, ears, nose . . . everything seemed to be in its usual place. What could it be?

Finally he realised what had happened.
His tail! It had gone!

Poddy looked in all the places
he had been that day.

But it was no use.

There was no sign of his tail.

The only place that he hadn't searched was in Flora's case.
Maybe she had accidentally taken his tail to Gran's!

But he couldn't check until Flora came back home.
Poddy wondered when that would be. . .

The next day Poddy didn't feel like playing
in the garden. He was far too miserable.
It felt like Flora would never come home.

He was so busy crying that he didn't hear the footsteps
approaching the front door. Or the key turning in the lock.
But he did hear the little voice that said . . .

"Hello my beautiful boy!"

Then he heard something else. A sort of swishing noise.

He turned around,
and there, back in
its usual place . . .

. . . was Poddy's tail.

Flora must have had it all along!